THE DETECTIVES OF NEW YORK

GAUTHAM KRISHNA SHRIGUHAN

Made with ❤ on the Notion Press Platform
www.notionpress.com

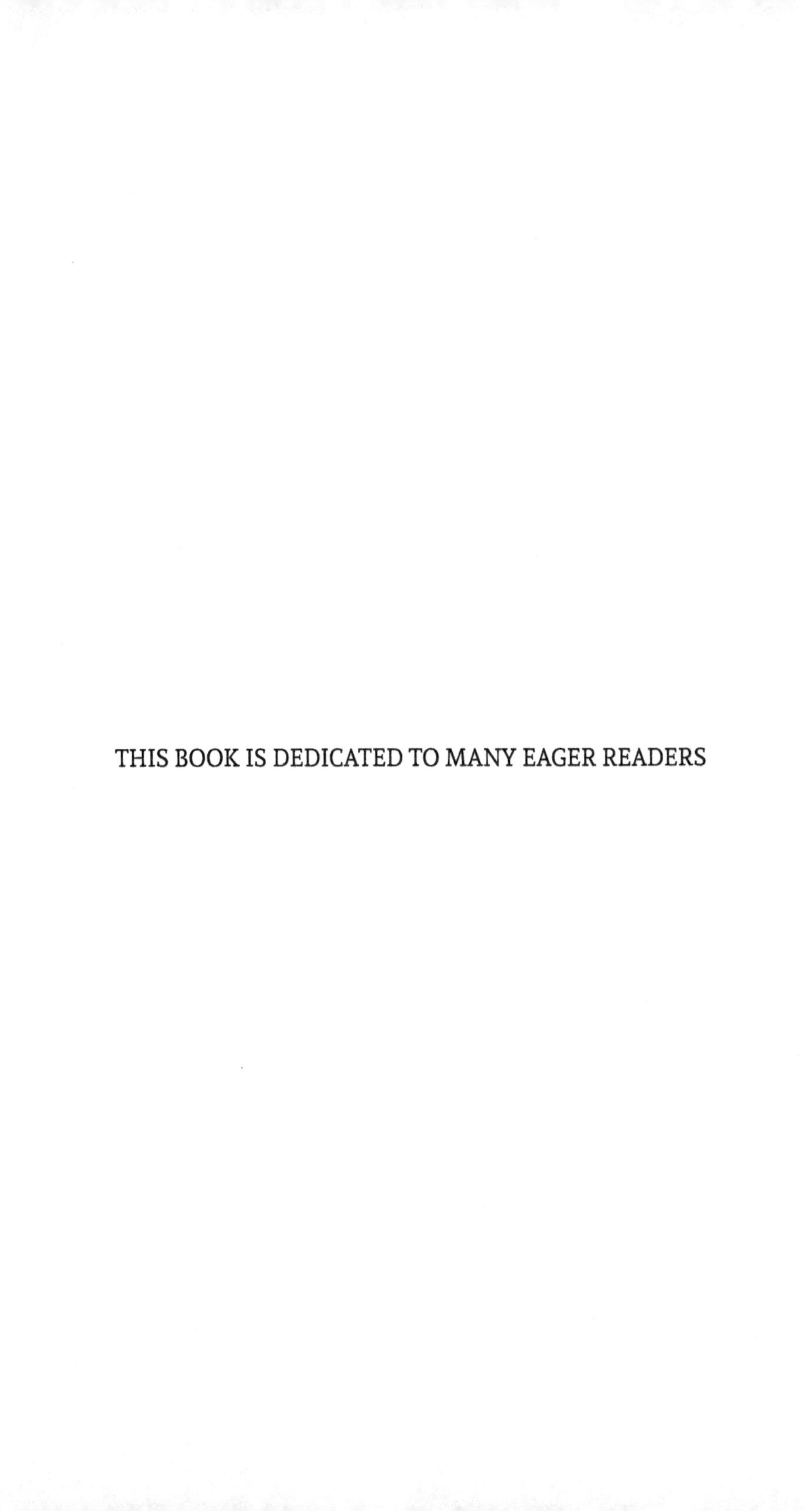

THIS BOOK IS DEDICATED TO MANY EAGER READERS

Contents

PROLOGUE

Joe, Peter and Edward are detectives in the city of New York, they have a very dear friend named Gustin, who is working in the top class order of FBI. They even have an innocent friend, who is a painter named Williams. The only con of the detectives is "Too late detectives", says Gustin for the three hundred and forty second time in his life. These five are very best friends from their childhood and are very talkative.

Preface

"I need a thriller crime story to read.", says many eager people in many abroad and even in our country. My intention to write this short detective book is to give a contrast to many people that "No devil can break friendship" . This thriller crime story is a story that shows in some places, even the FBI's can't be trusted, whereas the true friendship never breaks forever. I wrote this book to show a ultimate crime story to the people who asked me to. Basically, it's not my intention to write blood or fighting scenes in the story at this age, but it's just creativity of the young minds which help them to become a author due to the eagerness that builds up in the middle - aged people. Hope you like this book, grab some snack and start reading!!

I
The Start

The detectives felt very sad after hearing the sad news of their friend William being killed and stabbed. FBI officer, Gustin calls them over for the investigation. "So let's gear up for the mission", said Peter

&

So, when all set, they started their Honda Civic with full revving in neutral gear, and they started their journey to the place where William had been murdered. After Some time, When they stopped for a red light, they saw a very strange man, wearing a mask. He was holding a knife with some blood in his hand. "Hey, Edward, this man looks very strange and that too, he is having a knife with some blood in his hand. " said Joe. "Yes, let's go over there and give it a check. " said Edward and when they stepped out of their car and went near him, he got onto his heels and started running. " Hey! Hey! Stop right there. " shouted Peter but he ran away and so they got into the car and went at a very high speed and soon they were out of sight of the man. "Everything is very strange" said Joe. " and a bit confusing too" , added Edward. So, again they began their journey to New Jersey where William had been murdered. After a 2 hour tedious journey, they reached the site.

ರು

Gustin showed his FBI Officer ID and the officer took them inside. There, they saw the marks of the body and Peter started to examine it and he felt that, "These marks look like William had fallen from a very high place. " Joe and Edward felt the same way. But when they asked the nearby officer, "No, it can't be true because we have checked all the reports and it tells that the murderer has used a blade to kill him. ", replied the officer. All of a sudden, the officer got a phone call. He attended the call and he was astonished. "Hey, what happened?" asked Joe continuosly, but he didn't reply but after a minute, he had a massive heart attack and died

II

Falcon's Blackmail

The detectives were very astonished to see the officer die in front of them. "I think we should check the call log of the officer's phone, because he died after he had heard something very strange over the phone. " So, they rushed back to check the phone of the police officer.

When they saw the call log, they saw a strange number and they made a call to the number. It was ringing and someone with an aggressive voice answered the phone and they asked about the what he told to the officer that made him to die. The man replied ," I am a police officer and I told him that someone had killed his son using a knife and that is true." The detectives felt sad about the officer's son and all of a sudden Peter got a brainwave, "Hey, guys do you remember we saw a man near the traffic light, he was having a knife in his hand. ""Yeah, let's find a way to track him. " said Joe "But, what about

William?", questioned Edward "Don't worry Edward, maybe the killer of the officer's son could have killed William too. ", answered Joe and consoled Edward's sad mind.

ॐ

So they went to the same area, where they saw the man. There they saw the same man hiding behind the garbage bin, trying not to get insight of the officers or detectives. But, the detectives were too smart, that they found the man and finally caught the man and took them to "THE DETECTIVES OF NEW YORK OFFICE".

ॐ

There, each Detective took turns to question him.

"What's your name?" asked Peter

"Falcon"

"Why did you have a knife in your hand?" asked Joe

"My boss told me to do so. "

"Why?" asked Edward

"I don't know. "

"Who is your boss?" asked Peter

"Sorry, I can't reveal it."

"Then, did you kill the officer's son or William?. " asked Edward

"No "

"Ok Falcon, now you should take us to your boss or else we'll beat you up. "

But, Falcon was a bodybuilder and he could easily tear the ropes that had tied to his hands and feets and he ran away. "Do you think that Falcon might have murdered William or the officer's son?" asked Joe "Of course", replied Peter. So they informed the FBI officers and they took hold of Falcon and they threatened him that they would kill him if he didn't take him to his boss.

ೞ

Falcon took them to a very odd place and he said, "This is the home of my boss and he had gone out. He will come soon, " and told them to wait inside the place. The officers sat and very soon Falcon bought many weapons and killed every one of them.

III

The Secret Clue

After some time, the other FBI officers found out that the FBI officers were dead inside the house where Falcon led them. The detectives were very shocked to hear this. "Everybody are getting killed because of us. " said Joe sadly. When they got into the car, they were very shocked to see that there was an odd piece of paper on the seat of the car. "Hey guys , see there, there is a very odd paper on the seat, let's open it. " said Peter. Joe opened it "You can never find me." , was written on the paper. The detectives were very shocked to see the paper. They went to the same place where William had been murdered.

℠

There, they were very shocked to see the same thing written near the body marks. "Hey guys, let's check the handwriting of the text written in the paper using signatures signed in the police records. " said Edward. So, off they went to the nearest police station to check the handwriting.

❧

But the police didn't allow the detectives inside. Gustin had gone back to New York for some latest robbery case. So they went to New York to fetch Gustin to show his FBI ID to the police officer and the detectives told everything to Gustin.

❧

But, Gustin had to do some important investigations about the robbery case in Los Angles and could not come with the detectives. Now the trouble for the detectives starts. They have to find a new FBI friend to go and check the handwriting. The officer near Gustin's table was a man named James. He was extremely helpful to the detectives and a very kind hearted man. The detectives came with James to the police station in New Jersey and he showed his FBI ID to the police station.

❧

So they searched for the handwriting and finally found one that exactly matched the handwriting written on the odd piece of paper. It was found in the criminal list and his name was Kennedy.

IV

Is It Kennedy?

The detectives found the name written as Kennedy, "Maybe, we should look for the mobile number of Kennedy to contact him," said Edward. So they went to a man named Mathew, who had a job to track a mobile number of the name of a person given by his customers.

&

The detectives told Mathew to find a man named Kennedy, but now Mathew demanded a bulk amount of money for the process. But the detectives did not have enough money for the process. So They went to the nearest bank to get some loans.

&

After some time, they gave the amount to Mathew for the process. After a long scratch of time, Mathew informed the detectives about the phone number of

Kennedy. And Peter dialled the number and it was Kennedy who answered the phone, "What do you need, Peter. Are you surprised that I knew your name? " said the man. "Hey! Who are you?" asked Peter "Just turn back. " said the man and the detectives turned back and there was a man with a pistol in each of his hands and the detectives turned front and there they saw Mathew with a knife in his hand.

V
Will Edward Survive

The detectives ran away, except Edward, who was a slow runner due to some breathing problems that occured to him in his early age. Kennedy shot Edward in his leg and Edward was struggling with the bullet in his leg. But if the detectives tried to save him, they would also get shot by Kennedy, so the detectives ran away sadly.

The detectives got inside the car, "We should save Edward, but how?" asked Joe. Nobody had the answer for that. After some time, they went to the same place where Edward was shot. Thankfully, Kennedy and Mathew were not there, but the detectives saw Edward. Joe carried Edward on his shoulder and took him to the car.

They went to the nearest hospital and admitted him there. Peter got a call from the bank about the loan. They asked for the installment for the present month. Peter had transferred the money to the bank. Luckily, he had enough money needed for Edward's surgery. After some time, Peter paid the bill for the surgery. But now, he did not have any money left in his hand. "Don't worry Peter, I will fetch you some money, you do not need to meet all the expenses yourself for the case " said Joe. After some time, the surgery had started and the detectives were very nervous about Edward, mainly Peter as they both were best friends from their childhood and that too, Peter and Edward were cousins. The surgery was completed after some time, and the detectives went inside to see Edward. But Edward could not walk steadily for 2 weeks. So he had to use the walker. Peter was so pleased only after he saw Edward. Edward was to discharged from the hospital only after 3 days. Everyday Peter took good care of him by doing small helps like buying food, buying medicines and was a good speaker which generally made Edward improve. After 3 days, he was discharged and they continued their investigation.

ଓ

They got inside the car and with James, they went to the nearest police station. As the detectives were so smart, Joe had a hidden GoPro inside his shirt pocket, which no one could spot. Joe showed the footage of his GoPro which showed Kennedy and Mathew to the police officer. That night, the senior officer decided to hire a few professional officers, who should hide, where the detectives met Kennedy and Mathew. In the late night, the professionals heard footsteps and they spotted Kennedy. The next moment, they shot him in his leg and admitted him to the hospital.

ಇ

After some time, they investigated him.

"Why did you shoot the detectives?" asked the officer

"I can't tell." replied Kennedy

"We have legal rights to shoot you Kennedy, so tell me." said the officer and showed the shooting order to Kennedy.

Kennedy was scared.

"Wait wait, I will tell you sir, I am the boss of a gang which kills people, if they didn't give the money we asked for. " said Kennedy

"But why did you tell the truth?" asked the officer

"Because, I am not Kennedy." replied Kennedy.

Just then a nurse from the hospital in which Kennedy was admitted, came running and said that Kennedy had escaped from the hospital. The officer turned back to Kennedy and it was written that it was just a speaking robot.

VI
Peter In trouble

The detectives got to know about the incident and they remembered about Kennedy's mobile number that Mathew gave them. Then Edward got an idea "We can keep track of Kennedy's mobile number using the officer's number tracking device." ,said Edward. With this method they kept track of Kennedy using the mobile number tracker. After some time, they got into the car to track Kennedy. Finally after some time of pressing the accelerator to its best, they spotted and stopped Kennedy and finally took hold of him and they questioned him.

&

"Where is your gang?" asked Peter, "Attend your call first. " replied Kennedy. Just then the Mobile of Peter rang at it's loudest volume and the detectives closed their ears and eyes and Kennedy ran away in a minute. He attended the call and it said "Hello Mr. Peter, sorry to disturb you, I called you to pay this month's installment of the loan. " But this time, nobody had money with them. Peter cut the call. Luckily, James had the shooting order with him and the next moment he aimed his gun at Kennedy as he was easily spotted, even though he ran at his fastest speed. And finall he shot at Kennedy several times to confirm his kill. "Hey, why did you kill him? How can we find his gang?" asked Joe anxiously. "Listen guys, we can call Mathew and tell if he did not tell the criminals of the gang we will kill his family. We will call from a different mobile number." replied James. So they bought a new sim and dialled Mathew and Mathew attended the call and James threatened if he did not tell criminals of the gang, he would kill his family. But, in the meantime, the bank employees came to Peter as he did not pay the loan money and he was taken to the court and the judge ordered 6 months imprisonment.

VII
Falcon's End

Mathew was clever. He recognised the same voice when they asked the number of Kennedy. "Ok, go ahead, kill my family", said Mathew. But, really James had the order for killing his family, if he didn't tell about the criminals. So, now, he had to find the place of his family. He went to the police station to search and trace the address of Mathew and his family. After many hours of searching and sneezing because of the dust that came from the documents, he finally found the address of Mathew.

He rushed inside the car and travelled to the address that was found on the documents. He saw the house and went inside. He told the family that "Everybody, listen to me, I am going to do a video call to Mathew. I need dolls resembling each of you looking like real persons and when I shoot them, blood should come out from them and even a screaming noise. If you do not obey me, I have shooting orders to kill you, so obey me.". The family did the same way as James instructed them. And he called Mathew and showed a gun near his child doll's head and said "So, Mathew shall I kill him?" "Ok" said Mathew in a clear voice. Then James shot the head and blood came out and a screaming noise too was heard which the child had been told to make. Now Mathew was really scared. He believed James and immediately told all the names of the criminals of the gang and told him to leave his family. So James left the place and got into the car to find the criminals.

&

He went to the same traffic light zone, when the detectives were on their way to New Jersey. Now he saw Falcon walking in the street. He informed the other police officers about everything, when he turned again to see Falcon, he was not there. He had that noted that James saw him and he was standing behind his car and as Falcon was a bodybuilder, he lifted the car in his hand and crushed it into thousand pieces. Thankfully, when Falcon lifted the car, James could feel it and the next moment, he got out of the car. Falcon saw James out of the car and chased James. The police reached the place on time and James got into the car of the Police and they accelerated at a very high speed. After some time, James took over the wheel as Falcon was nearing them. He crossed the speed limit and police officers informed the traffic police to keep all the toll gates, bridges and railway crosses open as they were crossing the speed limit. The traffic police understood the situation and informed everybody about the disaster. After some time, Falcon was getting tired and he couldn't breath after that and so he fainted on the spot and before they could take him to the hospital, he died.

VIII
James At A High Risk

They finally escaped from Falcon and they had to go for the next gang member. To their surprise, it was their best friend, Gustin. They went to New York to catch him. There they went inside the same police station, but Gustin was not there. Mathew had told him to hide in a place, where James could not find. James asked the nearby officer about where Gustin had gone. "I do not know sir," he replied. At that time, James was alone. All of a sudden, a man pierced a knife in the neck of James. The man was Gustin. After some time, the police officers recognised him and admitted him to a hospital.

He was in a very serious condition and received intense treatment. It took more than 3 months for James to recover. In the meantime, Peter was freed and he came to see James in the hospital. "Hey James, who was the guy who pierced you?" asked Peter, "I think it was Gustin, I could not see properly after I was pierced."

said James. Peter, at once, went to the police station and ordered all the police officers to watch every area of New York from midnight till the next morning.

ೞ

Finally, in the morning, one of the very professional police officers got Gustin and brought him to Peter. "Hey Gustin, how can you betray us? We were friends from our childhood, how can you do this to us? Ok now I can not do anything. Get inside the cell." said Peter. After some days, The judge ordered 15 years of imprisonment for Gustin.

ೞ

After some days, when Joe went to the hospital, the doctor felt very sad to say that James had died. The detectives felt very sad for their dear friend. All of a sudden, Edward asked for the death certificate of James, but the doctor had a bad expression on his face and did not reply. "Did he really die or not?" asked Joe. Then he dragged the doctor to the police station and found out that his name is Oliver and he is also a part of the gang.

ೞ

He asked Oliver about James. But he was so stubborn that he would not say anything about James. Finally, an officer helped Edward to get a shooting order for Oliver. Then Edward showed the shooting order to

Oliver who was too scared for his life and told everything about James and where Oliver had hidden him. Then the judge ordered a 20 Years imprisonment for Oliver.

৪৩

Now they went to the place, where they saw James fully tied with many ropes. They removed the ropes. Now, they had to find only one person, Mathew, who was a clever man. They went to start the car but it did not start. Instead, smoke came out of the engine. Peter knew the reason for this and told everybody to run away from it and told them that Mathew had poured water in the engine oil tank . After some time the car exploded.

IX

Harry's Taxi

Now, the only car they had has exploded. Without it, they cannot travel anywhere. They had to buy a new car. They took a taxi to contact the car dealer. But, the taxi driver looked very odd, "Hey, where is your license, insurance policy and ownership certificate? You have to show it to us.", asked Edward. But, the driver did not respond. Instead he kept on driving to a very strange place. And finally, he stopped at a very dark and strange place. He got out of the car and locked all the doors.

&

"Hey, where are you going? This is not the place which I mentioned." said Joe. "I think the driver is Mathew" said Peter. Luckily, Edward had a hammer with him. All of a sudden, the detectives felt as if they were going upwards. They realised that the man had been using a crane to lift the car. After some time, they found out that the name of the man was Harry by seeing the driving license in the car's dashboard and he was also

part of the gang.

⅋

The next moment, Edward smashed all the doors of the car. But, it was too late. They were scared to jump out of the car at a very high height. Peter had a portable safety air bed. Then everybody jumped out of the car after using the safety air bed. But, before they fell on it, the man punctured the air bed. Now they cannot do anything except everybody should land on the man. So when they all landed, many bones of the man got fractured and the man screamed and died because of that itself.

X

Mathew's Attack

Now, they decided to take no risk and walked to the nearest car dealership. There, they saw a very handsome car. But it was offered for a cheap rate. "But, how?" asked Peter. "This is very strange, should we buy it?" asked Edward. They paid the money and went inside the car and it looked very strange. All of a sudden a faint spray appeared in front of them and it sprayed on them.

After they woke up, they looked around and it was a very strange place. All of a sudden, a man came out of nowhere, it was Mathew, Joe had a gun with him. The next moment he shot Mathew. But, it was just a doll like James did to Mathew's family. Real Mathew was in front of them, and behind him, there were hundreds of nuclear weapons. Peter heard a sound like the ticking of a clock. Just then they realized that there was a time bomb tied on everybody's hip

XI
The Grand Celebration

The detectives were very fearful. The time shown was "5:00 minutes left". Edward had known how to remove a time bomb. "First cut the red wire and the blue one and finally the yellow one.", said Edward. They did the same as Edward told them, but instead of defusing the bomb, the time started to run fast. Now, there was only one option left, that was to snatch the keys which could open the attachment of bombs onto their hips. They had to snatch the keys from Mathew or else this will be the end of the detectives. Mathew was turning back from them and was talking to another gang member about the robbery case in Los Angles which Gustin was acting like he was investigating about it, on the phone. Now it was Peter's turn to snatch the key from Mathew. He secretly went near Mathew's pocket and searched for the key, but it was not there. Then Mathew took notice of what Peter was doing. James had a gun in his pocket. The next moment, he took it out and shot

Mathew. Peter then took the keys of all the people from Mathew's shirt pocket and unlocked and detached the bombs as soon as they could and ran away from that place. They finally went to the car dealer and bought a real car for a normal rate and they drove to New York happily with a song playing in the musicbox of the car.

⁗

"Finally, we caught all the criminals of the gang." said Joe joyfully. They got out of the car happily to receive the medals and cash prize. Just then a man came running out of his house and he was running straight to them and he told the detectives that his name is Louis and he wanted to learn from them how to become a detective. The detectives happily accepted Louis as a student for them and the detectives went inside to receive the cash prize and medals. After they had received their medals, they headed to the Grand Celebration Hall, where all the officers were dancing and singing in joy of finding all the criminals and the detectives too joined them.

XII

Louis In The Gang

After a few days, the detectives started to teach Louis. That night, the detectives allowed Louis to sleep in their home itself as he had got hurt and could not walk much. Actually, Louis is an unmentioned criminal from the gang. So he decided to attack in an indirect way. That night, when the detectives were sleeping, he crept inside their room and used the secret method of detectives which they taught him.

But, the detectives heard the footsteps of Louis and they woke up. Louis hid in a cupboard in their room. The detectives flashed a torch all over the room to identify who is present in the room. After some time, they turned off the flash and continued sleeping. Then Louis walked very softly. So the detectives couldn't hear him. He went near the detectives with a knife. Everybody were asleep except Peter who was awake and was keeping an eye on Louis. Louis couldn't see in the dark without his glasses as he had forgotten to wear them. So he did not see Peter's eyes open. Peter waited to see what was happening. Louis was nearing and Peter decided to act as if he was a ghost. So he went near Louis and said "Hey, Louis, go away from here or else I will eat you!" and Louis was scared and ran away from that room and went to his bed to sleep.

ʕ

The next day, Louis asked Peter "Is there any ghost wandering around the house? Yesterday, I think I saw a ghost.". Peter laughed but did not reply, because he knew that it was himself who acted as a ghost. Louis was confused. Again, that night he came with a knife and this time Joe was awake and was keeping his eyes wide open and Louis again forgot to wear the glasses. This time Joe acted as a ghost when Louis was nearing. "Hey Louis, didn't I tell you yesterday that if you come here, I will eat you, go away!" shouted Joe and so Louis was extremely fearful and ran away. That morning Louis left the house in fear and all the detectives knew that Louis was the last member in the gang. They had noted the phone number of Louis when he had joined the detectives. The detectives gave the number to a man who works like Mathew, but not like Mathew.

ʕ

The man tracked the number and gave them each minute details and they drove their new car at a very high speed and the tracker showed that Louis was exactly right to them, when they turned right they saw the car of Louis. Then they realised that he had left the phone inside the car and ran away. But, the detectives easily found Louis running inside a narrow alley and they caught him.

XIII
The Final Judgement

That day, Peter called James over to arrest Louis. Then he took Louis to the court and the court ordered 10 years imprisonment for Louis and the judge also ordered to give a huge amount of cash for William's family. After some days, the detectives really started a home school to teach small kids about the techniques of detectives. Now, James has resigned his FBI officer post and now "The Detectives Of New York" is a four member group with James too.

THE END

www.ingramcontent.com/pod-product-compliance
Lightning Source LLC
Chambersburg PA
CBHW020331180726
47991CB00019B/1192